Hi, my nan
I'm twelve years o
of writing this book. I live in
California. It's been a dream of
mine for the past few years to write
and illustrate books about some
of my current interests in science,
sea animals, amphibians, reptiles, birds, endangered
animals, Minecraft, and more! I read many books on
these subjects, watch videos, play Minecraft in creative
mode, sketch, and draw in 3D and with the computer.

This is the first book in the Adventures of the
Axolotls series and follows my series of books on the
Curious Axolotl in Minecraft. All of my new ideas
quickly turned into the stories that I began putting on
these pages. I hope that you enjoy reading about the
axolotls' expedition to the Mushroom Islands as much
as I enjoyed writing about it!

I'd also like to say, "Thank you." Thank you
to my parents, Nana, Rhonda Asbenson, and the
wonderful teachers throughout the years who continue
to guide me in realizing my dreams and expressing my
ideas through writing and art.

Adventures of the Axolotls: Expedition to the Mushroom Islands in Minecraft

Follows the series The Curious Axolotl: Adventures in Minecraft
Written and Illustrated by Hayden Coles

This book follows the Mojang commercial usage guidelines:

- This book is not an official Minecraft product and is not approved by or associated with Mojang.
- Mojang has no liability for this product or purchase.
- This product's seller and manufacturer/publisher is not Mojang, not associated with, or supported by Mojang.
- All rights (including copyright, trademark rights, and related rights) in the Minecraft name, brand, assets, and any derivatives are and will remain owned by Mojang.

Published by Dougy Press
dougypress.com

ISBN: 979-8-9853820-7-5

Contents

CHAPTER 1

LIFE ON THE SEA

I suppose this expedition began a while back when the Sniffer and I started our mission to find Geode and Blurple, two legendary axolotl adventurers. Along the way, we met an axolotl named Citrine who helped us on our journey. We traveled through countless rivers just to reach the legends' base. Once we had snuck inside the base, we met Doug, a fellow adventurer.

You see, those adventurers don't travel alone. They always have Doug by their side protecting them and helping them on their expeditions. That actually makes a lot of sense, since we axolotls cannot stay out of the water for more than five minutes or so.

I think a human teammate like Doug is a great thing, so when we finally got to meet the two adventurers and quickly became part of their team, I was doubly excited!

Our first adventure on the team will be to retrieve a chest from the Mushroom Islands. This chest protects important information about the islands and the resources they contain, which will benefit Doug and all of us on the team.

A chest was the logical place for Geode and Blurple to store papers since they came to the islands without Doug and had no way to bring the papers safely back to the base.

We — Blurple, Geode, Doug, Citrine, the Sniffer, and I (Andesite) — left Doug's makeshift dock and have been at sea for a couple of months. We axolotls travel alongside the ship, always at the surface so we can easily talk with Doug. He had considered building us an aquarium so that we could ride on the ship, but we prefer swimming through the open ocean's waves.

We chat about what the Mushroom Islands could be like, and Geode and Blurple enlighten us since they have already been there. The Sniffer rolls along the creaky deck amusing himself as we chat, probably disappointed on the inside that there is no place onboard for him to enjoy his favorite pastime of sniffing for his precious seeds.

While the Sniffer slumbers below the deck, every night Doug goes up onto the deck to fish. He fishes until sunrise, keeping his finds in a barrel. Occasionally, he reels in other things like enchanted books or nautilus shells. Aside from these, most of his catch is cod or salmon with the occasional tropical fish, which he discards due to their inedible nature.

When he is done fishing, Doug trudges back to the cabin to begin cooking the fish in his furnace. Some days when it is particularly stormy and difficult for us axolotls to hunt, Doug has a few fish left over for us to eat. Of course, the Sniffer doesn't need to eat anything, showing no interest at all in the fish.

As far as fish hunting goes for us axolotls, we usually hunt during sunrise or noontime when the fish are the most visible among the kelp forests. We try to find a kelp patch where we can hide and wait for an unsuspecting fish to swim out into the open. From there, it's an easy catch for the day.

We have faced many storms along our voyage that have poured dense rain onto the ship, but this morning the sun is hidden by dark, menacing clouds, far worse than anything we have previously seen.

"This is gonna be a bad one. Not sure if the ship'll survive," Doug says jokingly, looking toward the horizon.

At that moment, a bolt of lightning cracks from one of the clouds, arcing across the sky toward what seems like a small island up ahead. The Sniffer shrinks back into a corner of the ship when he hears the loud, threatening thunder. Doug turns around and starts to pull in the sails, but Blurple points something out on the dark horizon.

"Hmm, am I seeing things?" Blurple asks, squinting and focusing hard on the storm's edge.

"Huh?" Doug questions, turning back around toward Blurple.

"I swear I saw something get lit up by the lightning. Like a ship or something."

"You're probably still seeing things. Remember that ghost you allegedly saw in the base last year?" Geode teases.

"I saw it!" Blurple shouts back angrily.

"Calm down. I'm trying to study where we are on this nautical chart right now," Doug complains, wiping rain from his face.

"It's not one hundred percent accurate. I hope it'll get us to the Mushroom Islands, though I don't think your ship will make it all that way," Geode jokes.

"Very funny. Be quiet now; I'm trying to focus," Doug replies in a serious tone.

The ship goes quiet for a couple of minutes. The silence is only interrupted by the occasional crackle of thunder and the sniffling of the Sniffer. Then, there is a distant clicking somewhere on the side of the ship.

"Does lightning make clicking sounds?" Citrine asks.

"Uhhh, I don't think so," Doug replies. "I hear those clicks, though; not sure what they are."

Then a fin rises from the rough waves.

"Whoa. Okay, okay. There's something in the water," Citrine says, frightened.

"It's a fin. Do they have sharks around here?" I ask.

"No, dummy, I hope not," Blurple says jokingly.

"Am I just seeing things? That's not one fin; they're three of them!"

We hear more clicking sounds followed by some sort of chirping.

"Those aren't shark sounds," Citrine says, holding onto the hull of the ship, trying to press himself as flat against the ship as he can in order to more easily blend in and go unnoticed by the "sharks."

"If it's a shark, then you'll be the appetizer!" Geode jokes.

"Quit it," Citrine replies, holding back laughter but shocked by what is in the water.

Two more fins rise from the sea, gently swimming away from the pack toward the ship.

Geode and Blurple suggest, "Come swim behind the ship with us. You'll be safe from those creatures."

Citrine hesitates following their advice until it's too late. "Ok, go now and hurry! Get me out of here!" Citrine screams.

The two water creatures gain speed rapidly, launching right for the bow of Doug's ship. Citrine shrieks and bolts away to the stern at the last second, and the two ram into the ship, rattling her!

"Wait a second. This seems oddly familiar," I say, remembering the dolphins I long ago used to sink my attackers' ships. "They're dolphins."

"Huh? Doesn't seem like it. Didn't think dolphins were supposed to torpedo into your ship," Doug replies.

"Well, I have no idea why they do either, but they're the only reason I'm here."

"Wait, Andesite; what do you mean?" Doug asks, confused.

"I'll tell you later when we aren't so occupied."

One of the dolphins chases Citrine through the rough seas.

"Help me! It's chasing me!"

Eventually, Citrine gets exhausted and stops to catch his breath, but the dolphin catches up to him. The creature gently nudges him before swimming away back toward the pod. Citrine looks at the fin and is confused.

"That thing chased me...just to nudge me?" Citrine wonders, befuddled.

"I guess so. They're strange creatures," Doug replies.

The dolphins ram into the ship one last time before losing interest in us and disappearing into the waves. Doug checks on the Sniffer to find him below deck, still huddled in the corner, startled by the loud thunder and the violent ramming of the ship.

Out of breath, Citrine says, "Well, that was surely tiring."

"Sure was. But I hope you have some energy in reserve. We should reach the Mushroom Islands sometime today according to the charts," Doug declares.

"As I've said before, the charts we made may not be completely accurate. You can only get so accurate when you're drawing it from memory. You know?" Geode explains, trying to be funny.

"Uh, sure, I guess," Doug replies. "Anyway, from what you remember, Blurple, does it seem like we're pretty close to those islands?"

"I think…I'm not sure, but this seems pretty familiar," Blurple replies. "Oh, wait. I know where we are. I see that island up ahead. It's close to the Mushroom Islands. We'll be there soon."

"What do we still have to do to get to the Mushroom Islands?" Citrine inquires curiously.

"Well, it seems like we're gonna have to turn starboard soon, but after that, it's smooth sailing straight to the islands," Blurple clarifies.

"Hmm, that island isn't the one we are after. It's far too close to be a Mushroom Island unless this chart is giving out false information," Doug says, frowning. "The islands should be a few hundred blocks from here, so…right *behind* that island, it seems."

The team falls into silence for another couple of minutes, the rain pattering on her deck. As large waves slam into her wooden hull, Doug rushes over to the bow of the ship with his charts, the floorboards creaking.

"These waves are huge! We might have to land on that island 'til the storm passes."

Suddenly, the ship's hull rattles with the cracks of breaking wood.

"What's going on down there?!" Doug asks, shouting over the heavy rain.

CHAPTER 2

THE STORM

"There's a big hole on the port side! Get down here and help me! We need to stop as much water coming in as possible. Come on guys!" Citrine yells.

Doug storms down the wet stairs, losing his footing and sliding into the water. Blurple and Geode approach the damaged part of the hull and are swept quickly into the ship as water floods through the hole. They desperately look for their good friend, but to no avail. We don't see either of them for a few seconds, but Doug eventually gets up, and we notice a large welt forming above his eyebrow. Doug wades through the rushing water, struggling to get his gear out.

We notice that the Sniffer is nowhere to be found, but we hear creaking from above and realize that the Sniffer is running about on deck getting hit by the dangerous waves! Doug has no time to help the Sniffer to safety; by the time he gets out some planks to repair the hole in the hull, the water level has risen over his head!

Doug gets to work, filling in the gap with his spare planks, and we all can only hope that the Sniffer settles down soon.

"Guys, I need more planks. Try to keep as much water from coming in as possible while I get more wood from the chests on the deck," Doug instructs, rushing back up the flooding stairs.

Blurple, Geode, Citrine, and I build an axolotl wall of sorts with our bodies, covering the majority of the hole, hoping to slow the flooding water a bit.

Doug returns minutes later with a couple more spare planks. He fills in the remaining gap before going back up to the deck to check on the Sniffer and assess the damage.

"She'll floa…"

Another crack rings out, this time from one of the masts. Doug looks up as the mast splinters in half, the top arching toward the deck. A massive wave crashes into the ship, hurling the broken mast straight into the deck! Shreds of what used to be the sail scatter over the broken ship, and the Sniffer hurries to the stairs to flee below deck!

We now start to worry about Doug. He hasn't been seen since the mast fell. A couple of moments later, he rises from the rubble and pushes the destroyed mast into the angry sea.

The storm lasts for a few more hours, continuing to damage the ship, but eventually, the storm ends its reign of terror and blows off to the south. The damage has already been done—a broken mast beyond repair, ripped sails, and a hole in the hull that hasn't been completely fixed.

"I think she'll float. We'll have a harder time getting to and from the islands now without one of our masts," Doug says, further assessing the damage. "Well, let's see. We're one mast down and have one patched hole in the hull. Most of the other damage seems to be minor. Cracked floorboards…those can easily be fixed."

Doug continues assessing the damage. "The only thing I'm worried about is how far we are blown off course by the storm. It could be days or even weeks before we reach the Mushroom Islands."

Doug hoists the remaining sails on the surviving mast, which unravel to show many holes and tears. With the last tattered sails hoisted, we continue onward at a much slower pace.

Over the next few days, Doug spends his time going down to the flooded hull, hauling buckets of water up and dumping them over the side of the ship back into the sea. Every day that he bails, the ship rises a little higher out of the sea, now not weighed down by all the flooding.

We eventually find ourselves in the Warm Ocean. The water here is as the name suggests, much warmer than the rough waters we had previously traveled through.

"Now that we're in the Warm Ocean, the Mushroom Islands must be close, right?" Doug hopefully asks Geode.

"Yeah, part of the islands are in the Warm Ocean. We should be close to the chain now. I think we've gotten back on track since the storm hit, and now all we can do is hope and wait!" Geode says excitedly.

A few long hours later, the sun illuminates the caps of massive mushrooms as it sets below the horizon.

"There they are!" Doug exclaims. "We'll get there by midnight if we're lucky."

"Doug, we should wait until the morning to reach the islands because Blurple and I saw lots of sandbars the last time we were here. It's too risky to travel at night this close to the islands," Geode explains cautiously.

"The sandbars aren't marked on the charts," Doug replies, looking the charts over one more time. "Now that I know that the sandbars are there, I won't sail these waters at night."

Doug drops anchor, and we sit out the night until morning comes. I decide to take a quick nap by the hull until dawn.

I awake from my slumber to the warm sunlight filtering through the waves. I crawl out of sleep and wake up Citrine, who had decided to sleep on the ocean floor by a couple of kelp vines. When we reach the surface of the water, we can see the Sniffer lying on his back on the deck, his moss illuminated by the sun. We also see Doug walking toward the side of the ship to talk to us.

Yawning, he asks, "Are you guys hungry?"

"Sure, I could use a few fish before we get back to adventuring," I reply, but Citrine stays suspiciously quiet.

"Ok. Here, catch," Doug says, throwing a few cod overboard toward me.

I secure the cod and begin to eat one. It seems like I am the only one hungry for fish, but it couldn't be further from the truth. Citrine snatches one of the fish from me, sneaking away with my food back down to the seafloor.

"Hey, Citrine, who said that you could take one of my fish? You're not gonna get away with this!"

"Who says I can't?" Citrine responds.

"That's a valid point," I murmur to myself.

"I'm just playing with ya," Citrine calls out, but I continue to chase after the thief.

He hides the fish in some kelp before turning around to face me.

I confront him, "Why do you always steal? Every time I get my food, you always take some for yourself. Why can't you just ask Doug for some?"

"I don't know. I thought it was funny."

"Wow, such a great response. I'll let you have that fish, but no more."

I swim back up to the surface to see my stockpile of fish gone except for the fish I had been eating.

Doug walks over and says, "Sorry, I forgot to feed the others; I guess they stole from you. I would give you more fish, but I don't have any extra."

I eat the remainder of the cod in silence, disgruntled by the fact that the others had stolen from my stash. I am quickly distracted from my frustration though when Doug weighs anchor and the ship is on its way. We slowly make our way toward the Mushroom Islands again.

"Andesite, now that things have quieted down a bit, I keep thinking about what you said when we were getting rammed by the dolphins. Why did you say that dolphins are the only reason you're here?" Doug inquires.

"It's a long story, but I was getting attacked by two men who were standing up in their boat. A pod of dolphins happened to be swimming by. I lured them close, and they rammed into my attackers' rowboat, throwing my enemies into the ocean, sinking their boat, and allowing me to escape!"

Geode and Blurple swim up to us. "We're getting pretty close to those islands. It feels like it has been a long time since we saw them, I must say," Geode declares excitedly.

"I'll get ready to drop anchor!" Doug says, full of anticipation.

CHAPTER 3

EXPLORING THE MUSHROOM ISLANDS

Excitement fills us as the Mushroom Islands come into view. As we approach the first island, waves crash against its rocky coastline with the surf propelling us along. Through the ocean spray, I catch a glimpse of the Sniffer jumping into the water to wade through the rough waves. We swim through the shallow breakers of this, the largest of islands, as Doug's damaged ship slowly approaches the shore.

Citrine and I eventually find ourselves in calmer water and soon realize that we have stumbled into a cove whose entrance is hidden by the ocean spray. We rush back to the boat to inform Doug of the place to drop anchor where the water is calm.

As Doug maneuvers his boat through the harsh waves and ocean spray to the cove, Citrine guides the ship into the narrow entrance of the calm and secluded waters while I wait with the others.

Fortunately for Doug, the cove seems to be deep enough for his boat, and he throws the anchor off the hull into the salty waters. The large anchor sinks to the seafloor, scraping across the rocky seabed as Doug grinds the ship to a halt. He grabs his essentials from a chest and leaps off the ship onto the island's gray earth.

He jumps backward, bumping into the ship in shock. The ground feels like no other ground he has walked on before, but he adjusts to the unusual feel of the special dirt pretty quickly.

As I swim closer to shore, I notice that this strange soil is truly *strange*. It seems that tiny spores have risen from the ground, something I've never seen before. The ground is damp, but unlike dirt, it is *spongy*.

Doug prods at the soil with his sword before pulling out a shovel and digging up a square block of the gray mass. He suddenly turns his head to look at something…something moving. We can all see it— the patch of moving mushrooms.

They walk in groups, trodding over the gray hills in front of us. One moving patch seems to call out at one of us in a deep voice, but what it says is unintelligible. As the groups move closer, I can't help but notice that they look oddly familiar, but I can't put my finger on why. As they amble toward us, it becomes obvious. These are cows infected by the mushrooms, but not harmed by them.

"We saw them when we arrived on our first expedition. They're cows, that's obvious. But we couldn't figure out why they had been covered in mushrooms! We tried to lure one over to figure out why, but without being able to go on land for very long, it was practically hopeless," Geode explains.

"It was difficult enough to bury our chest. It took hours of 5-minute trips in and out of the water," Blurple adds.

Just then, the Sniffer appears from some shallow water and hops over to a group of infected cows. He sniffs them and tries to play with them, but they pay no heed to his actions and continue with their life. He then mopes back to us, his wet moss clinging to his back.

He lies down and tries to bury his head into the gray earth but quickly pulls his head up, clearly dissatisfied with the ground. He won't sniff around in this soil because of the unusual texture and the lack of seeds. The Sniffer then stands up, more disappointed than ever about the island that he traveled for three months to reach.

We move from the serenity of the cove to the harsh coast where we first reached the island, traveling along until we notice a brown spire, unlike any other mushroom we have seen on the island so far. And as we get closer, it becomes all too clear what it is: a shipwreck!

Within the rocky shoreline, a long mast juts up from an unexpected sandy beach. The mast has been snapped in half with time. It seems obvious what happened—a sailor must have beached his boat into the sandy shore, unaware of the dangerous island he sailed directly into. Or maybe the ship was damaged by a sandbar, and in a last-ditch attempt, the sailor tried to drop anchor, but instead the ship crashed into the shore.

It is an eerie sight, and it becomes even more grim when I realize that this could've been Doug's ship torn to pieces just as this hull was destroyed by the sharp rocks on the shore. I shake that out of my head. We are all safely on the islands now; that is all that matters.

Doug climbs onto the shipwreck's creaky deck, part of which is still intact. What isn't so intact is the hull, which has been ripped open in several places. Doug explores the beached ship's insides that are scattered around the wreck of the ship. He comes back with multiple finds, some of which get my attention. One is a chart, ripped in one corner but surprisingly unscathed, even though the hull is open and water is getting in.

"Hey, Doug. I'm wondering why this chart is so intact since it was in a shipwreck," I shout over to the wreck.

"Huh?" he asks, crawling out of the hull, "Why what? I didn't hear what you said."

"Why is this chart undamaged?"

"Oh, I found it in a chest with some other stuff, like gems."

I murmur to myself, "That chest would've already flooded if it had been in there for so long. Maybe this shipwreck isn't as old as we think."

Doug continues, "There's lots of stuff here. I've already found 21 gold bars, and I'm trying to open up this heavy chest that probably has more. I've found more than a stack of emeralds and diamonds already. These weren't sailors; these were pirates!"

"And by the looks of it, this shipwreck is fresher than we think. Think about it. Those chests would've already been flooded, and that chart would've already been soaked. I have a bad feeling about that wreck. Whoever those pirates were, they had companions — companions that could be trying to find them right now," I explain to Doug.

"You're right. I think it's better that I leave the rest of the treasure I haven't uncovered yet in the ship's wreckage. We should find the chest that Geode and Blurple buried before those pirates come back to fight us," Doug says almost jokingly as he gathers up the riches he already found and puts them into his pack.

"Hey, Geode, where's that chest you guys buried?" Doug asks.

"Oh, I'll show you. It's pretty close. Follow me."

Doug, Citrine, the Sniffer and I follow Geode and Blurple as they lead us to the chest that is the motivation of our expedition. We are excited and proud of how far we have come and all we have endured to reach our goal.

"Now if we go over here…" Geode says, leading us over to a small beach. "Ok, this is where we buried the chest."

Geode points to a particular part of the beach. Doug pulls his shovel out of his pack and begins digging a hole in the wet sand. I marvel at how a person like Doug can help us axolotls at key parts of our adventures.

The sand flings all over us, and the Sniffer jumps back to avoid getting it in his eyes. Doug has found our chest!

The Sniffer clearly sees that something important is taking place, and he leans forward to get a closer look. We quickly swim to the edge of the water to try to get as close as possible. Geode and Blurple look as excited as usual, though they are the ones who buried the chest and don't lean in as closely as the rest of us do.

Doug slowly unfastens the chest's already rusty latch, and we peer in with eager anticipation!

CHAPTER 4

CHEST OF SECRETS

D oug pulls out a small piece of wrinkled paper from inside the sandy chest, slowly reading what it contains. He looks back and forth from Geode and Blurple to the paper a couple of times with satisfaction.

Doug is already satisfied with his first glance into the chest, but the treasure is not as impressive as I had expected. I guess the true treasure is in the beneficial information and resources the chest contains for Doug. I had thought that the treasure chest would hold many riches like gold bars and various jewels; I had been wrong.

"It's good to know you can use these mushroom blocks as a fuel source. I usually use lava buckets, but these could be helpful as well. Say, how many things can you smelt with a mushroom block?" Doug asks the two axolotls with a twinkle of interest in his eyes.

Geode whispers to Blurple, "Uhh, I don't think we wrote it down. You can smelt 2 things, right?"

Blurple murmurs nervously, "I think so…Let's just say that."

"We think it's around 2 blocks or so. Not as useful as lava, but what if there's no lava around? Then I guess the mushroom blocks could be a lot more useful than you expect," Geode explains.

"Hmm, what's this?" Doug asks himself, pulling out a bowl of something. "Not sure if I want to taste that quite yet."

"It's mushroom stew. Try it; I'm sure you'll enjoy it," Geode replies, gesturing toward the soup.

Doug takes a small sip out of the bowl, trying to swallow it. "Tastes a bit earthy, wouldn't you say?"

"Yeah, Geode doesn't like it. He thinks it tastes like dirt," Blurple says.

"It does," Geode replies.

Blurple adds, "He doesn't like stews. He doesn't think a bunch of food should be all mixed together in a bowl."

"That's not true; I like suspicious stew! Half of the time at least. Remember that time when you tried to poison me with that stew? I knew it didn't smell right," Geode replies grumpily.

"No, I did not try to poison you," Blurple says, looking for approval around our group. "It was just a joke. You didn't even drink it."

Sometime during the stew discussion, the Sniffer lost interest in the chest and trotted off to smell the dirt.

Doug intervenes in the axolotl stew battle declaring, "Stop yelling. It says here that you can make potions with the mushrooms, though I guess the only useful potion you can make is invisibility. All the rest deal damage or slow you down in some way. I'll make a couple of invisibility potions for us right now," Doug says, pulling out his brewing stand.

"The mushrooms help with making the fermented spider eyes, but I think you need a night vision potion and fermented spider eyes to make an invisibility potion," Geode replies, remembering more details. "I am beginning to think that what is in this chest is a more important treasure than I had originally thought."

"According to this recipe, I guess the only thing I wouldn't normally have is those mushrooms because I never encountered them on any of my journeys before. But now I have," Doug says, collecting a few brown mushrooms from the gray earth nearby for his pack, probably to start a mushroom farm at his home to give him a regular supply.

Doug picks a couple more mushrooms and mixes them with some sugar and spider eyes he had rolling around in his pack. He makes some fermented spider eyes, which he puts into his brewing stand. He then pulls out a handful of spare night vision potions, which he slots into the three empty spaces on his stand.

The potions turn from bright green to a clear color in mere moments. Doug reaches for a bottle but pulls his hand back quickly.

"Should've waited for the potions to cool down!" Doug exclaims, wincing in pain.

We wait for a couple of minutes until Doug bends down and feels one of the potions to find that it is cool enough to handle. He then continues to remove the two other invisibility potions from their stands. He stashes them in his pack alongside the other various potions there. It's hard to believe that Doug had gone so far in his adventures without these invisibility potions!

Doug sorts through the chest, pulling out a couple of bottles of weakness and harming. "These aren't that useful though. Why did you guys put these in here?"

"Well, you can use a weakness potion to cure zombie villagers," Blurple says, trying to explain.

"That doesn't make much sense. How can weakness cure something?" Doug inquires.

"Let me explain," Geode says, jumping into the conversation. "The first step is to give the zombie villagers golden apples. Then splash them with weakness. I'm not sure why, but then the zombie villagers apparently get cured and restored back into normal villagers. We're still trying to figure out why, but we think it has something to do with weakening the villagers so the effects of the golden apples are more pronounced."

"That's cool. I haven't run into a zombie village yet, but when I do I guess I can use this to cure some of them," Doug says with ideas floating around in his head. "That's not all—because after you cure that villager, its trades will be lower than when…"

An arrow whooshes by, narrowly missing Doug's face! He turns around, expecting a skeleton, but instead, he is met by another arrow bouncing off of his armored shoulder. Doug quickly throws his harming potion at the incoming attackers. A person falls to the ground, dropping his bow and clenching his stomach.

Doug approaches the person carefully, sword in hand. It seems he tries to make peace with the archer but is taken by surprise when a powerful blast of air launches a mace-wielding barbarian straight toward him. He brings his mace down, barely missing Doug.

Debris flies into the air, and Doug is shot back toward us. He lays still for a few moments before standing up.

"Hey, you two! Take these potions and get away as fast as you can!" Doug yells, throwing the splash potions onto Citrine and me, giving us the effects immediately.

"And you guys," he calls to Geode and Blurple, "Escape from here and hide somewhere, maybe under my ship if the attackers haven't destroyed it!"

"What about the Sniffer?" I ask desperately.

"I don't know. I'll try to protect him. I'm sure he'll be fine."

With that, Doug pulls out a crossbow, loaded with what seems like a firework for an arrow. The last I see of the firework, it explodes into a blast of color as it collides with the macebearer. I duck beneath the surface, hiding from the incoming rain of arrows. I swim to deeper water as several arrows pierce through the surface, leaving a trail of bubbles behind.

As I escape the battlefield, I realize it is hard to process the fact that we have been attacked—by other people, of all things. We axolotls can't defend ourselves against these attackers, and all we can do is watch as Doug is charged by these raiders.

Hoping that the Sniffer is okay, I look for the others but see no sign of them except for Geode's tail, faint in the distance. I turn around and try to follow him, but he is already long gone. I am all on my own now, just as I was when I left the Lush Caves long ago.

I decide it will be good if I can find a shelter, such as a shipwreck or one of those ruins. There are a lot more things that want to attack me here in the open ocean than when I was with Doug and the others.

Faint explosions can be heard in the distance, but I don't try to go back to save Doug. Without weapons, the most I can do is cheer him on as the

attackers barrage him with arrows and potions. I turn
my head and notice faint lights in the distance.

That is strange. I've never seen anything like this
underwater building before. I approach slowly, wary of
any dangers that may lie within.

I won't go back to the islands. I am worried
those people will see me, and so I decide I will
explore whatever this building is in front of me. As
I approach, I feel strange…watched. I turn around
quickly, but nothing is there. Maybe I just feel like I
am being watched, but maybe I'm not actually being
watched at all!

As I continue onwards, I look to see any signs of
one of the axolotls. Geode went this way; he must have
seen this place. Soon, the whole building comes into
view. Giant green pillars rise from the gravel, holding a
massive building off the seafloor. A grand entrance lies
in front of me, lanterns lighting up the murky water.

Out of the corner of my eye, I notice movement
by one of the building's walls, but I dismiss it for
sea kelp swaying in the ocean surge. I decide that
whatever's inside is safer than the outside, where I am
susceptible to being attacked by all sorts of creatures.

I swim through the entrance, instantly feeling
a cold rush of water on my face. All sorts of small
congested tunnels seem to lead to other parts of
whatever this building is, but I pick a smaller section

overgrown with kelp and seagrass. Chiseled ocean bricks line the walls with the same lanterns from outside lighting up the tight space.

After checking outside and realizing that the sun has gone down, I decide to go to sleep in the cramped space where I am temporarily making myself at home.

I awake to a sound early in the morning. I open my eyes and notice bubbles floating around the front of my room. I pay no heed to the bubbles but notice something large hiding in the corner as I move to exit the small room.

The creature turns around in an instant, revealing its massive eye! It seems to be covered in lethal spikes, and I swim away toward the exit as fast as possible. Its eye glows for a moment before shooting out a laser directed right for me!

CHAPTER 5

MISSING THE SNIFFER

I feel a sharp pain in my back, throwing me to the ground and forcing me to momentarily halt my escape. I get back up and quickly exit the building, the green creature far behind, remaining back to guard the entrance as it glares at me.

I hide behind a small sandbar, peeking over my shoulder to make sure I am not being followed. Looking back to the building's entrance, I see a couple of those guardians looking threatening, probably trying to stop me from coming back. Staying at the scene any longer, I realize, will be risky. So I take off for some islands that hopefully will be safe enough for me to stay for the next couple of days. I think about the Mushroom Islands. Those were safer than being around one of these buildings.

Not knowing where the raiders are worries me, but there's no way that their fight with Doug went through the night, so I see it as a good time to return.

Without knowing where the islands are, it takes days of traversing the rough waves to notice distinct mushrooms on the horizon. As I approach, I hear no sounds of explosions and swords clashing together. The battle is surely over. Now the only thing I'm worried about is who won.

As I reach the island's rocky shore, my heart sinks as I notice a familiar person resting against a mushroom stalk.

"Doug. Doug! Are you there? Are you all right?" I shout to him, worried.

"Yeah, Yeah. I'm all good," Doug mumbles.

"Did you win?"

"Yeah, but I got sliced in the arm. I'm fine. Trust me," he says, holding onto his wounded left arm.

"Why don't you look happy then? At least you won, right?"

"See, the thing is, I couldn't protect the Sniffer and fight them at the same time. I decided it would be best to get the attackers off the island. It was only after I had succeeded in forcing them off that I noticed that they had taken the Sniffer."

I feel regret, even heartbroken. If I hadn't left, maybe I could've led the Sniffer away from the battle to somewhere safer.

"What can we do about the Sniffer?" I ask.

"Well, we can't just leave him out there in the wild with those attackers. I'm not sure what they'll do with him. I guess we can try to find him. Do you agree?" Doug says, pondering deeply.

"Of course, I agree! There's no way I am leaving the Sniffer with those awful people. Where are the others? Did they come back yet? They can help us rescue the Sniffer, too!"

"Only Geode and Blurple have come back. They're relaxing somewhere. They said they saw Citrine somewhere after his effect wore off. He might be coming back soon."

As I say this, I notice a familiar head pop out of the water.

"Oh! Well, there he is!" I say, truly surprised.

I realize that nearly all of our team is assembled. Now we can try to find and save the Sniffer from those people!

"How are we even supposed to figure out where they went?" Citrine asks with a confused look.

"I'm not sure, but the attackers couldn't have traveled very far since the battle. I would guess we should look around the islands, because how would they even know that these islands were here unless their base was somewhat close?" Geode inquires, thinking deeply.

"Didn't we include some other islands on the chart?" Blurple asks, trying to picture the chart in his head.

"And why would we do that?" Geode seriously questions Blurple.

"I don't know. So Doug wouldn't crash his ship into them? You were the one who drew them on the chart," Blurple replies.

"Guys, stop arguing. I have the chart. I'll pull it out," Doug says, unraveling the chart from his back pocket.

The axolotls bump into each other, both trying to get a better look at what Doug is seeing on the chart.

"See! I told you. You added those other islands," Blurple says with much pride.

We examine the chart for a couple of moments, trying to find any islands that seem like a logical place to make a base. Eventually, Citrine says that he had tried to follow the attackers' ship for as long as his invisibility effects would take him. He says he remembers leaving a certain part of the island, and after concentrating for a couple of minutes, he remembers roughly the place their ship launched.

We make our best estimate of where that is on Geode and Blurple's chart. By making a line from this point, we notice a couple of islands that seem pretty convincing as the cover for a secret base, and so we decide that these are the isles to check out first.

I ask Doug, "How long do you think it will take for us to get your ship ready for sailing?"

"The attackers completely destroyed it."

Honestly, I have been thinking we are good to go to hopefully save the Sniffer. But something I hadn't considered is that the attackers destroyed Doug's ship. Without the ship, travel to any of these isolated islands will be extremely difficult for him. I'm not even sure Doug could do it; he always says that he is not very good at swimming.

A new worry floods my mind: Doug being stranded on the island without any way off. Because the island is barren of any significant resources like wood, which could be used to make shelter, we are not sure how long he could survive.

The other issue with Doug being stranded is that he is a significant part of the effort to rescue the Sniffer. After discussing it with the other axolotls, I realize that because we aren't able to be on land for as long as he is, Doug is THE crucial part of us being able to save the Sniffer!

Maybe Doug can make a cheap boat out of a few planks, though one of those boats could only take him so far. The storms will probably destroy its weak frame far before he would ever see the sight of the attackers' base.

Days go by as we try to come up with a plan, exploring many different ideas as the hot sun glares down on us. Doug uses the beached shipwreck as shelter and a way to avoid the sun's burning beams of light. The nights are easier than the days. The heat vanishes at night, and because the island is devoid of mobs, we can peacefully sleep.

One day, Doug has a particularly good idea. After inspecting the beached shipwreck, he finds that even though it is damaged, it is still salvageable. He makes it his mission to restore the shipwreck to its former glory for sailing the rough seas. I'm surprised we didn't come up with the idea sooner.

I feel at peace realizing that Doug might not be as stranded on the islands as we originally thought.

Maybe the Sniffer can be saved after all, and if he can, maybe we can rescue him soon!

CHAPTER 6

OPERATION: RESCUE THE SNIFFER

Doug quickly begins scooping the nearby sand from the shipwreck into one large pile since he needs a better look at what needs to be done. He explains to us that we will play a crucial part in securing the ship to sail on the rough waves. His game plan is to dig a large trench under the tilted ship with the starboard side facing upwards. The bow will then point toward the sun during the early hours of the day.

His next step is to let the trench fill with water so that the ship will be afloat, allowing us to finally leave to rescue the Sniffer.

"How long do you think it'll take?" Citrine asks. "If we take too long, I'm not sure what they will have done with the Sniffer by then. Maybe they will have moved him."

"I'm not sure either; the most would be a couple of weeks. As far as the plan for restoring and launching the ship goes, execution is key. If we get the process right, maybe we can leave for the Sniffer in 9 days," Doug says, tallying his fingers to count how much time each step will take.

"Welp, we better not waste much more time talking. Talking doesn't do anything," Geode adds restlessly.

Doug starts by digging a border around the area where the ship had crashed into the beach before using his trusty shovel to scoop the sand off and away from the starboard side of the hull, allowing him to tilt the ship into a somewhat upright position.

Doug next builds makeshift scaffolding using some leftover bamboo scraps that he found in a storage chest on the ship. He says that the scaffolding should keep the ship upright while he makes repairs and when we later dig through the sand to connect the trench to the sea.

It seems as though we can start digging the trench now, but Doug reminds us that he still needs to fix those small damaged areas in the ship's hull first to prevent the ship from filling with seawater.

Soon his repairs are done, and it is time for us to take over the project. Our main job is to extend the trench from the ship to the ocean. Then the hole will naturally fill with water, allowing the ship to float through the trench opening to the sea.

Doug has already loosened the larger rocks which will make digging the trench much more straightforward. With that, the rest of us start work on our part of the project. I know that if something goes wrong or we mess up, Doug probably will not be as forgiving as usual because both his and the Sniffer's survival are at stake.

Geode and Blurple remove all the small stones and pebbles to make digging the trench easier, and then Citrine and I step in to finally start digging. It is hard work; we aren't built for digging, and it's a lot more difficult underwater. Citrine is good at clearing away more sand faster than I can.

I scrape away at the sand, and the small waves help wash away the sand as I loosen it. Maybe the water will rush into the trench soon, and my job will be done. Though it feels like hours, I eventually see that I am getting closer.

But it seems like my luck is up when the last line of sand collapses into the trench, and seawater rushes in, carrying me with it!

As the cavity fills up, and a torrent of water crashes into the trench, I hold onto a large rock that hasn't been cleared out yet, narrowly avoiding getting thrown against the ship by the force of the incoming water.

After barely avoiding certain death, I quickly exit the trench and find my way to a place where I can see Doug on the deck of the ship. Doug is watching with anticipation as the trench fills and the ship floats up and begins to drift into the ocean.

While we all worry about the strength of the ship's repairs and whether she will be seaworthy or not, we are relieved to see the ship stabling itself out with the calm currents of the cove. Now, Doug has a stable ship that will allow him to escape from the desolate island, barren of any resources.

What was once a trip to the Mushroom Islands to find a chest became a fight for survival! I find it funny to think that to save Doug from the island, I had a close call with death as well! Soon, the Sniffer will be in good hands once again, and we can all return home. My worries aren't focused on simply escaping these islands; I want to save the Sniffer. Plus, getting to him sooner rather than later will be best.

It looks as if we will be leaving the islands far earlier than Doug originally predicted. While we are ahead of Doug's 9-day goal at the moment, we aren't in the clear yet. While he had all the materials to fix the hull using wood, he didn't have any wool or string on hand, which are essential to make the sails. Without these sails, travel on the ocean will be more difficult.

I suppose that we could come up with some paddles to propel the boat, but Doug will be the only one who can use them, and he'll tire too quickly to make paddles practical.

We find a couple of chests in a corner that we have yet to open. Doug opens up one to find dozens of maps and charts. While this chest might have seemed useless, I have an idea. By sewing these papers together, we should have just enough to make sails that will work!

After I give Doug my idea, he gets right to work creating the sail, attaching each map meticulously to another. While he is in the middle of the process, he notices that these seemingly unrelated maps actually have a purpose, and while he doesn't know what that can be, he works for hours sewing each map and trying to find their true function.

"I think I've connected the maps correctly. They seem to show a path through the ocean, stopping at several smaller islands until, I guess, the trail just stops at the Jungle Islands. I don't think whoever was on the ship made it all the way there before being shipwrecked, but that seemed to be their destination."

"The Jungle Islands? Are they close to this island?" Geode asks, trying to recall something.

"Let me check," Doug replies, walking back to the ship. A couple of minutes later he returns. "I mean, I guess they are close to where we are now. The islands look familiar though."

"Oh, wait. Aren't we going to the Jungle Islands after we leave this one?" Geode asks, finally remembering what he was trying to recollect.

"That's right; those are the only Jungle Islands in the area. Something is going on on those islands. We need to get there now.

Right now, I have more questions than answers. I'm not sure if there may be people waiting for us there. Maybe they're keeping the Sniffer there. We're going to have to find out," Doug says, looking very overwhelmed at what lies ahead.

CHAPTER 7

THE START OF A NEW JOURNEY

After fastening the makeshift sails onto the old wooden mast, the ship seems ready to ride the ocean's fierce waves as it once had. It took nearly a week to get the ship back in working order, and we are eager to get back on the water as soon as possible to rescue the Sniffer.

As we are preparing to face the Sniffer's captors, Doug brews us some potions in case we are ambushed once again. He makes a variety of potions, all with the purpose of protection.

These elixirs include more invisibility potions to help disguise us if we need to escape, regeneration to help us heal from potential attacks, and potions of healing to restore our health instantly. Although healing potions provide similar attributes to regeneration, they provide an *instant* boost of healing rather than regeneration's gradual healing over time.

Now we are geared up for a certain battle with the attackers.

Soon enough, Doug's new old ship is making its way past the cove into the rough ocean where he hopes the ship will weather whatever challenges come. Its sails seem to help push the ship along, but Doug notes that he can't reach the speeds that he once did in his old ship.

While the ship isn't performing as well as Doug had expected, according to the nautical chart, our journey to the Jungle Islands should only take a few days. It seems as if the Sniffer will be away from those attackers and in better hands soon enough. If it hadn't been for them, we could've just gone home and rested. It doesn't matter now; we are on course to rescue the Sniffer!

As we pass through the open ocean, I shudder. Something is off, and while I don't know what, something seems awfully familiar. Then I notice lights at the bottom of the ocean and realize now why I feel so scared!

Before the others can learn what the danger is, I hear a crack in the hull. Luckily, the crack didn't penetrate into the thick hull. While this has happened to Doug's previous ship, I don't know if repairing this ship will be so straightforward with the constant barrage of attacks from below!

The guardians I encountered before are a problem again! While we have no interest in their castle, they see our being here as a threat. Doug reaches for his gleaming sword and dives into the water. I peek below to see a massive battle starting far below with Doug already gaining the upper hand. He swings his sword, and it cuts through the water, its fine blade making contact with a guardian's armor. The guardian's scaled armor pulls in its spikes, seemingly ready for another blow, but Doug turns around swiftly and finishes him off by surprise and continues to take care of the rest!

The battle is over in mere minutes in Doug's favor. The army was decimated from a hundred to just a few who retreated into the ancient fortress. Why they had chosen to attack is unknown; whatever plan their minds had come up with had greatly backfired.

With our motivation and self-esteem at an all-time high, we take no heed of islands that seem to offer a safe harbor. We are on a mission, a mission to save our friend!

The next day, in the early morning sun, I am awakened by the distant shouts of something off the ship. I rub my eyes before ceasing to breathe to listen for whatever is talking. It can't be Doug; I know he couldn't be that far from the ship. I peek above the surface to see an island clouded in fog, but something stands out—another person.

I haven't seen any other people since the time Doug was ambushed, but I know that meeting these people comes with risk. If Doug tries to introduce himself, the man will attack him. Can it be the opposite—the man being friendly and accepting of Doug? We will have to find out!

As Doug drops anchor onto the rocky seabed by the barren island, the man runs forward desperately, his tattered and faded shirt waving in the wind.

"P-please, spare me something! Bread will work," he says, quivering.

"Who are you? Wait, you look familiar. Oh, so did they throw you overboard or something?" Doug asks.

"No, I fell off, and they couldn't find me. I swam here, to the closest island I could see."

"How did you just fall off the ship? Did someone push you off or something?" Doug questions.

"No, they're my teammates. It was raining and the deck was slippery. When I was trying to stabilize myself, I guess I just fell off. It should've been easy to get back onto the ship, but because of the rain, the others couldn't see me."

"That's too bad," Doug says almost mockingly. "You realize I'm not giving you food, right?"

"Why? I've done nothing wrong!"

"Oh, you've done a lot wrong. You're part of those attackers. I remember your face. Mace guy, eh?" Doug says, not hearing a word the man says.

"But, I'm a changed person! All I need is some food. You can't leave an innocent man here, you know.

That'll come back to bite you," the man says, trying to change Doug's mind.

"I wasn't going to leave you on that island. I have other plans for you. You've tried to attack me along with dozens of others of that group you're sailing around with. Come in here. I'm sure you'll like it while you live." Doug says, gesturing inside the ship.

"Uh, o-okay. This means I'll get food also, right?" the man asks frantically.

"No promises."

Doug turns to us and says, "We'll be having a new guest with us for a little while. He'll have his own room, and if he tries to talk to you through the porthole, ignore him. Refer to him as Mace Man and nothing else. Understood?" Doug asks, trying to be as pleasant around the man as possible.

Something tells me though that Doug has worse intentions of what he will do with Mace Man.

Doug locks the man in a partially flooded cabin and goes back up on deck.

We ask Doug why we are letting the man who had attacked him stay on the ship. As usual, he says he has a master plan.

As our journey continues, Doug rarely visits Mace Man. When he does, he always brings some raw fish as food for the prisoner. Mace Man must be in a worse state than when we found him.

When Doug isn't visiting him, we always hear Mace Man attempting to escape. As he tries to break the floorboards, we can hear the scraping noises through the hull and into the water.

Finally, Doug tells us his master plan, which is a lot more clever than we were expecting and will make our journey to get the Sniffer back a lot easier. You see, he plans to hold the former raider captive in the ship until we find the rest of his team who have the Sniffer.

Because Mace Man is such a strong and crucial part of their team, when we offer to trade him for the Sniffer, the attackers will probably not be able to refuse. Plus, the state that Mace Man is in will surely make the attackers wary of what Doug could do to them.

One day, after hearing the unmistakable scraping of the floorboards in the hull for two hours straight, we notice something far in the distance. At first, I mistake it for a cloud, probably hanging low to the ground for one reason or another. But as we get closer, I realize first of all, that clouds usually don't get that close to the ground, and second, that what we are looking at is certainly an island, or almost certainly.

Large sprawling trees jut from its mountainous landscape mixed with thickets of bamboo. A large piece of land seems to hang over the island, seemingly defying physics. Streams of water flow from its edges, but most notable is something that shouldn't be there—a temple covered in moss and seemingly built centuries ago.

To the ordinary eye, a place like this might seem unfit for living, but to Doug, the dense cover and sloping overhang make this land a perfect place for a base.

As the ship rides through the tropical waves, and dazzling, brightly-colored fish swim by, it narrowly avoids the tall corals reaching toward the surface. Upon approaching the dense Jungle Island, I can't help but realize the challenging terrain and treacherous journey that lie ahead. But if we can save the Sniffer, then the journey will be worth it!

AXOLOTL FACTS

- Did you know that axolotls can live up to 15 years? These remarkable creatures have gills on the sides of their heads, and so the next time you see an axolotl, you'll know what those frilly things protruding from their heads are! Axolotls also can surprisingly regenerate limbs! For example, if one gets its leg bitten off by a predator, it can regrow another leg in its place in around 40 days, good as new.

- Axolotls come in a variety of colors but are known for being that famous pink. They also come in colors, such as blue, golden, and albino. Believe it or not, most wild axolotls are brown, like mud.

- Axolotls may seem harmless perhaps because of their everlasting smile, but these creatures are predators. In the wild, they hunt prey such as small fish, tadpoles, salamanders, and tiny crustaceans.

- Axolotls live in Lake Xochimilco and some rivers and canals by Mexico City. Due to people releasing large fish that eat axolotl eggs into these waterways, axolotls are becoming endangered. There might only be 1,000 left in the wild if we don't build protected habitats quickly. There are groups working day and night to do just that, and so supporting them will be very helpful.

- Mexico City hasn't forgotten about axolotls. In 2017, a contest was held to find 20 emojis for Mexico City to use. Some of the first place emojis were of axolotls! The people of Mexico are also helping by cleaning up trash in lakes and waterways.

- People have stepped up to the task, creating axolotl-safe environments where axolotls grow and live. We can help by donating money to axolotl conservation centers that will help keep these fun animals in the wild for decades to come. These special creatures deserve to survive!

See you in our next adventure!
**Adventures of the Axolotls:
The Temple**

*Andesite, Citrine, the Sniffer,
Geode, Blurple, and Doug*

Farewell

THE AXOLOTL
A 4-BOOK SERIES

THE AXOLOTL
ADVENTURES IN MINECRAFT

HAYDEN COLES

NOT AN OFFICIAL MINECRAFT PRODUCT
NOT APPROVED BY OR ASSOCIATED WITH MOJANG

THE AXOLOTL
ICEBERG ADVENTURES IN MINECRAFT

HAYDEN COLES

NOT AN OFFICIAL MINECRAFT PRODUCT
NOT APPROVED BY OR ASSOCIATED WITH MOJANG

THE AXOLOTL
NETHER ADVENTURES IN MINECRAFT

HAYDEN COLES

NOT AN OFFICIAL MINECRAFT PRODUCT
NOT APPROVED BY OR ASSOCIATED WITH MOJANG

THE AXOLOTL
BEATING THE ENDER DRAGON IN MINECRAFT

HAYDEN COLES

NOT AN OFFICIAL MINECRAFT PRODUCT
NOT APPROVED BY OR ASSOCIATED WITH MOJANG

FOLLOWED BY

THE CURIOUS AXOLOTL

A 2-BOOK SERIES

THE CURIOUS
AXOLOTL
THE NEW WORLD
ADVENTURES IN MINECRAFT

HAYDEN COLES

NOT AN OFFICIAL MINECRAFT PRODUCT
NOT APPROVED BY OR ASSOCIATED WITH MOJANG

THE CURIOUS
AXOLOTL
HUNT FOR THE TWO
ADVENTURES IN MINECRAFT

HAYDEN COLES

NOT AN OFFICIAL MINECRAFT PRODUCT
NOT APPROVED BY OR ASSOCIATED WITH MOJANG

ADVENTURES OF THE AXOLOTLS

A 3-BOOK SERIES

ADVENTURES OF THE

AXOLOTLS

EXPEDITION TO THE MUSHROOM ISLANDS IN MINECRAFT

HAYDEN COLES

THE
ALLAY
THE
FROG
AND THE
AXOLOTLS
ADVENTURES IN MINECRAFT

HAYDEN COLES

THE
GLOW
SQUID
ADVENTURES
IN MINECRAFT

HAYDEN COLES

THE
PARROT
AND THE
PANDA
ADVENTURES IN MINECRAFT

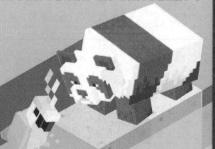

HAYDEN COLES

CHECK ONLINE FOR THE LATEST RELEASES
AXOLOTLSERIES.COM

HAPPY READING!

Made in United States
Orlando, FL
16 December 2024